Walter Satterlee, Kate Sanborn

Grandma's Garden

with many original poems - Volume 1

I0692617

Walter Satterlee, Kate Sanborn

Grandma's Garden
with many original poems - Volume 1

ISBN/EAN: 9783337090111

Printed in Europe, USA, Canada, Australia, Japan

Cover: Foto ©Andreas Hilbeck / pixelio.de

More available books at **www.hansebooks.com**

𝔉𝔯𝔞𝔫𝔨𝔩𝔦𝔫 𝔓𝔯𝔢𝔰𝔰:
RAND, AVERY, AND COMPANY,
BOSTON.

Contents.

3

CONTENTS.

THE OLD GARDEN.

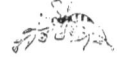

IT'S well enough: looks kinder knowin',
    Them red and yeller leaves and things:
They make a mortal sight o' showin',
    Some like a bird that never sings.

But birds to sing, and blows for smellin',
    Was what we had when I was young:
A patchwork quilt is jist as tellin'
    As them things on the grassplot flung.

You'd ought to seen my granny's gardin,
    With pinks as sweet as any spice,
And posy-beds she worked so hard in
    To keep 'em square and clean and nice.

Tulips — my land! their bright cups holdin'
    Right up to catch the sun and dew,
Purple and white and brown an' golden,
    And red with sunshine streamin' through.

And Canterbury-bells a-swingin',
　Dim blue like bits of April sky,
And dancin' columbines a-ringin'
　For every bee an' butterfly.

Crocus an' hyacinths an' daffy,
　Yeller as dandelines to see,
A-lookin' at ye kinder laughy,
　As though to say, "Why, here we be!"

And white narcissus, straight and slender,
　With rings of red fire in their snow;
And little snowflakes, just as tender
　As things that in a greenhouse blow.

And roses — my! that tall old white one,
　Milk with the sunrise in the cup,
And some most red enough to fright one,
　And pink, like sea-shells curling up.

Roses don't smell like them no longer,
　There's smoke an' bone-dust in 'em now:
Mabbe the bushes do grow stronger,
　But I'd as lieves they'd smell as grow.

And lilies — well, they was too splendid,
　All dazzlin' white, an' gold inside,
Jest as though Natur' had intended
　To make a blossom for a bride.

6

Oh, yes! I know your *Jap*-pan lilies,
  As big as p'inies, and as proud:
They smell — oh my! — and amaryllis,
  No smell at all, — a pretty crowd!

Give me the old Dutch honeysuckle
  A-makin' even the night-time sweet,
A-blossomin' at every knuckle,
  And hangin' to your very feet.

And pink and buff and white carnations,
  And rosebuds snuggled up in moss,
Heart's-ease and vi'lets, dear relations,
  And gay snapdragons, bright and cross.

Give me the good old week-day blossoms
  I used to see so long ago,
With hearty sweetness in their bosoms,
  Ready and glad to bud an' blow.

Well, well, I know them days is over,
  And I have lost my clear young eyes;
But can't I still smell pinks and clover?
  I tell you some things never dies!

Rose Terry Cooke.

OUR LADY-OF-THE-LILIES.

UR Lady-of-the-lilies,
    The valley-lilies fair!
Her brow was pure as any babe's,
    And silvery white her hair.

The snows of ninety winters
    Had fallen upon her head:
Within her clear, benignant eyes,
    A history sweet you read.

She walked among the flowers
    That her own hands had sown:
With lilies-of-the-valley white
    Her paths were overgrown.

Through the old grassy garden,
    Year after year they stole:
Their fragrance seemed the very breath
    Of our dear Lady's soul.

She gave away her lilies
    Freely as wild birds sing:
They bore to sick and lonely ones
    The first glad hint of spring.

Our Lady-of-the-lilies
　　Loved other blossoms too :
She was our Sweet-Pea Grandmamma, —
　　The dearest flower she knew.

With early heats of summer
　　Came forth the sweet-pea's blush,
Pink as the soft tint of her cheek,
　　Or sunset's last, faint flush.

And, clipping bud and tendril
　　In morning's dewiest hours,
Her thoughts on lovely errands ran, —
　　" Now who shall have my flowers ? "

Surely her love was in them,
　　Like sun and dew and air ;
For sweet-peas wonderful as hers
　　Blossomed not anywhere.

They crowded through the fence-rail,
　　They sprang to meet her touch,
All winged and waiting for a flight :
　　Where shall we now find such ?

And oh ! what fairer blossoms
　　Can grow around her feet
In that new garden where she walks
　　Within heaven's climate sweet ?

I think they must have brought her
    The dear old-fashioned flowers,
Before her heart felt quite at home
    Even in the angels' bowers.

"Our Lady-of-the-lilies,"
    Even there her name may be;
While here fond memories cling to her
    As Grandmamma Sweet-Pea.

                Lucy Larcom.

COUNTRY PLEASURES.

W E are too apt to judge of flowers, as we do of men, by their great names, or by some exterior and vulgar quality; or we like them because they are the fashion, and not by virtue of their own intrinsic sweetness and beauty. I have no wish to depreciate the splendid and ingenious productions of the modern florist, or to deny that a trim garden is a source of pleasure to me; but I like the old-fashioned flowers best. In the old English flower-bed, where only perennials with an ancient ancestry are allowed to grow, there is always delight; and I should be sorry to exchange its sweet flowers for any number of cartloads of scentless bedding-plants mechanically arranged and ribbon-bordered.

                George Milner.

THE GARDEN OF "AULD LANG SYNE."

—◆ ◆—

OH, far, far back, adown the years that stretch
 between the then and now,
 My memory turns, and I forget the lines of
  care upon my brow,
And feel myself a child again in grandma's garden,
 hard at play, —
That quaint old place where dwelt the lights and
 shadows of the summer's day.

I close my eyes, and seem to hear the drowsy hum of
 busy bees,
And catch the lullaby of winds soft singing through the
 maple-trees,
And, bordering the gravelled walk, by memory's aid I
 see once more
The dear old flowers grandma loved and tended in those
 days of yore.

The stately hollyhocks, which grew beside the lilies white
 and tall;
The wondrous sunflowers in a row beside the broken
 garden-wall;

The plump white snowballs rising from a nest of ribbon-
    grass around ;
The flaunting tulips standing guard so boldly o'er their
    bit of ground ;

The fragrant pinks, which mingled breath with the sweet-
    marjoram and thyme,
And watched their enterprising friends, the morning-
    glories, climb and climb,
Until they towered o'er the porch where grandmother
    was wont to sit,
To watch the humming-birds, and on her blue yarn
    stocking calmly knit ;

And oh the box ! that grew so green and sturdily beside
    the walk ;
The mint that grandma loved ; the fennel growing high
    upon its stalk ;
The "ragged-sailors" my young hands were fond of
    pulling all apart ;
"Sweet-Williams," and the "four-o'clocks," — oh, lovingly
    within my heart

I hold the memory of them all, and seem again to breathe
    the air
Of that old garden ; nor can modern hothouse perfume,
    rich or rare,

Make me long less once more to see the dear old friends
    of "Auld lang syne,"
When life itself a garden seemed, and care touched not
    this heart of mine.

Oh precious hours' of memory when backward I can turn
    my gaze,
And make myself a child again, happy in childhood's
    careless days!
Full many a joy returns to me, full many a vision
    bright; but oh
There's none so dear to me as grandma's garden in the
    long-ago.

                        MARY D. BRINE.

CHERRY-BLOSSOMS.

ENT was dreary and late that year;
    April to May was going;
But the loitering moon refused to round,
    And the wild south-east was blowing.

Day by day, from my window high,
    I watched — a lonely warder —
For a building bird in the garden-trees,
    Or a flower in the sheltered border.

But I only heard the chilly rain
    On the roof of my chamber beating;
Or the wild sea-wind to the tossing boughs
  . Its wail of wreck repeating;

And said, "Ah me! 'tis a weary world
    This cheerless April weather:
The beautiful things will droop and die, —
    Blossom and bird together."

At last the storm was spent. I slept,
    Lulled by the tired wind's sighing,
To wake at morn, with the sunshine full
    On floor and garden lying; —

And lo! the hyacinth-buds were blown;
    A robin was softly singing;

14

The cherry-blooms by the wall were white ;
And the Easter bells were ringing !

It was long ago ; but the memory lives ;
And in all life's Lenten sorrows, —
When tempests of grief and trouble beat,
And I dread the dark to-morrows, —

I think of the garden after the rain ;
And hope to my heart comes singing,
" At morn the cherry-blooms will be white,
And the Easter bells be ringing."

Edna Dean Proctor.

OUR GREAT-GRANDMOTHER'S ADIEU TO HER GARDEN.

O flowers,
That never will in other climate grow,
My early visitation, and my last
At even, which I bred up with tender hand
From the first opening bud, and gave ye names !
Who now shall rear ye to the sun, or rank
Your tribes, and water from the ambrosial fount ?

Paradise Lost, Book XI.

AN OLD-FASHIONED GARDEN.

N old-fashioned garden? Yes, my dear,
No doubt it is.   I was thinking here
Only to-day, as I sat in the sun,
How fair was the scene I looked upon,
Yet wondered still, with a vague surprise,
How it might look to other eyes.

'Tis a wide old garden.   Not a bed
Cut here and there in the turf; instead,
The broad straight paths run east and west,
Down which two horsemen could ride abreast,
And north and south with an equal state,
From the gray stone wall to the low white gate.

And, where they cross on the middle line,
Virgin's-bower and wild woodbine
Clamber and climb at their own sweet will
Over the latticed arbor still;
Though, since they were planted, years have flown,
And many a time have the roses blown.

To the right the hill runs down to the river,
Where the willows droop, and the aspens shiver;

And under the shade of the hemlock-trees
The low ferns nod to the passing breeze;
There wild flowers blossom, and mosses creep,
With a tangle of vines o'er the wooded steep.

So quiet it is, so cool and still,
In the green retreat of the shady hill!
And you scarce can tell, as you look within,
Where the garden ends, and the woods begin;
But here, where we stand, what a blaze of light,
What a wealth of color, makes glad the sight!

Red roses burn in the morning glow;
White roses proffer their cups of snow;
In scarlet and crimson, and cloth-of-gold,
The zinnias flaunt and the marigold;
And stately and tall the lilies stand,
Like vestal virgins, on either hand.

Here gay sweet-peas, like butterflies,
Flutter and dance under summer skies;
Blue violets here in the shade are set,
With a border of fragrant mignonette;
And here are pansies and columbine,
And the burning stars of the cypress-vine.

Stately hollyhocks, row on row,
Golden sunflowers all aglow,

Scarlet poppies, and larkspurs blue,
Asters of every shade and hue;
And over the wall, like a trail of fire,
The red nasturtium climbs high and higher.

My lady's-slippers are fair to see,
And her pinks are as sweet as sweet can be,
With gillyflowers and mourning-brides,
And many another flower besides.
Do you see that rose without a thorn?
It was planted the year my Hal was born.

And he is a man now. Yes, my dear,
An old-fashioned garden. But, sitting here,
I think how often lover and maid
Down these long flowery paths have strayed,
And how little feet have over them run
That will stir no more in shade or sun.

As one who reads from an open book,
On these fair luminous scrolls I look;
And all the story of life is there, —
Its loves and losses, hope and despair.
An old-fashioned garden — but to my eyes
Fair as the hills of paradise.

JULIA C. R. DORR.

MY GRANDMOTHER'S GARDEN.

Y grandmother's garden! how well I remember
    That spot that delighted my eyes when a boy!
From the balm-breathing June to the mellowed
      September
I hailed its fresh blossoms each morning with joy.

In fancy I see it when eve dark and chilly,
    O'ercasting the city, forbids me to roam:
In memory blossoms the rose and the lily
    When solitude freshens the pictures of home.

I seem on the garden-gate swinging and singing,
    Or on the bars leaning in summer eves long;
And, waiting my father his team homeward bringing,
    I list once again to the whippoorwill's song.

I remember the porch where the woodbine in clusters
    Of billowy green o'er the white roses hung;
The swallows, whose purple and emerald lustres
    Shot swift through the air where the orioles sung.

O'er the old mossy wall, in the mellow airs blowing,
    The lilacs made fragrant the evenings of May;

And close by the door where the house-leeks were
　　growing,
　My grandmother's garden, my pleasure-ground, lay.

A-near was the orchard, the moss to it clinging,
　The home of the birds and the banquet of bees:
There oft, when the Whitsuntide church-bells were
　　ringing,
　Like hills of red roses trees flamed over trees.

My grandmother's garden with green box was bor-
　　dered;
　There bloomed the blue myrtles, the first flowers
　　of spring;
There the peony's leaves seemed with pansies embroi-
　　dered;
　And hands of the fairies the bluebells to swing.

The balm-bed was there; the sweets from its flowers
　The humming-birds, gemming the air, came to draw:
And peeped from the woodbine and jessamine bowers
　The hives of the honey-bees golden with straw.

There oft, with her hymn-book, my grandmother wan-
　　dered,
　Then seated herself in the arbor alone,
And read the old hymns, and on holy themes pon-
　　dered,
　While long on the hilltops the western light shone.

20

They are gone, all are gone, whom that garden once
    gladdened:
No more shall I see them, — the young or the old:
Nor my grandmother's face with long memories sad-
    dened;
    Her crown of bright silver is changed into gold.

Dimmer light have the springs and the summers that
    follow;
    The charm of the roses is not now as then;
In duller-gold skies flits the purple-winged swallow:
    My heart ne'er will feel its old freshness again.

The joys youth expected were lost in the winning;
    The distance enchanting from death's door is gone;
And life a lost thread, like the firefly's, is spinning:
    I am lonely at night, and am weary at morn.

But oft, with emotion that time doth not harden,
    I turn to my old home, its lessons recall;
And the brightest of scenes is my grandmother's garden,
    Its pansies of spring, and its asters of fall.

And wherever I roam, in whatever bright harbor
    The anchor may drop, I remember with joy
The prayers that in summer-time rose from the arbor
    In that blooming garden when I was a boy.

HEZEKIAH BUTTERWORTH.

AN OLD-FASHIONED GARDEN OF OLD-FASHIONED FLOWERS.

EN having said that half the parish had mounted on a hay-rick close by to look at my garden, which lies beneath it (an acre of flowers rich in color as a painter's palette), I could not resist the sight of the ladder, and one evening, when all the men were away, climbed up to take myself a view of my flowery domain. I wish you could see it! — masses of the Siberian larkspur and Sweet-Williams (mostly double); the still brighter new larkspur, rich as an Oriental butterfly — such a size and such a blue! — amongst roses in millions, with the blue and white Canterbury-bells (also double), and the white foxglove, and the variegated monkshood; the carmine pea in its stalwart beauty; the nemophila, like the sky above its head; the new erysinum, with its gay orange tufts; hundreds of lesser annuals; and fuchsias, zinnias, salvias. geraniums, past computation. So bright are the flowers, that the green really does not predominate amongst them.

To MISS BARRETT.

THREE-MILE CROSS, June 20, 1842.

My dear Love, — I write to say that on Saturday next we shall send you some flowers. Oh, how I wish we could transport you into the garden where they grow!

You would like it, it is so pretty. One side, a hedge
of hawthorn, with giant trees rising above it beyond the
hedge, whilst all down within the garden are clumps of
matchless hollyhocks and splendid dahlias; the top of
the garden being shut in by the old irregular cottage,
with its dark brick-work covered with vines and roses,
and its picturesque chimneys mingling with the bay-tree,
again rising into its bright and shining cone, and two old
pear-trees festooned with honeysuckle; the bottom of the
garden and the remaining side consisting of lower hedge-
rows melting into wooded uplands, dotted with white
cottages, and patches of common. Nothing can well be
imagined more beautiful than this little bit of ground is now.

Huge masses of lupines (say fifty or sixty spiral spikes),
some white, some lilac; immense clumps of the enam-
elled Siberian larkspur, glittering like some enormous
Chinese jar; the white-and-azure blossoms of the variegated monkshood; flags of all colors; roses of every shade,
some covering the house and stables, and over-topping
the roofs, others mingling with tall apple-trees, others
again, especially the beautiful double Scotch rose, low but
broad, standing in bright relief to the blues and purples;
and the Oriental poppy, like an orange lamp, for it really
seems to have light within it, shining amidst the deeper
greens; above all, the pyramid of geraniums, beautiful
beyond all beauty, rising in front of our garden-room,
whilst each corner is filled with the same beautiful flower,
and the whole air perfumed by the delicious honeysuckle.
Nothing can be more lovely.

MARY RUSSELL MITFORD.

A SOUTHERN GARDEN.

HE house was of brick, large and commodious; and flanked by neat out-houses and servants' quarters, presented an imposing appearance, an air of lordly beauty. The shade-trees were forest-born, — the maple, oak, beech, and, fairest of all, the tulip-poplar. Excepting in the greenhouse, on the south side of the mansion, and a rose-creeper that climbed upon the piazza, not a flower was tolerated within the spacious yard; and the sward was always green and smooth.

In the garden, beauty and utility joined hands, and danced together down the walks. There were squares of thrifty vegetables, deserving a home in the visioned Eden of an ambitious horticulturist; and the banished floral treasures here expanded in every variety of hue and fragrance. The enclosure was well stocked with fruit-trees, currant and raspberry bushes; and at the angles formed by the straight, broad walks were clumps of lilacs and snowballs (their stems hoary with moss), thickets of cinnamon and damask roses, white and red, or, standing up erect and stiff, a calycanthus-tree. There grew the dwarf lilac and the jessamine family, — the star, the Catalonian, the white and yellow, — thatching one arbor; while the odorous Florida, the coral, and the

24

more common but dearer garden honeysuckles, wreathed their lithe tendrils over another ; and ever-blowing wall-flowers, humble and sweet, gaudy beds of carnations, brightly-smiling coreopsis, and pure lilies with their fragrant hearts powdered with golden dust, — a witching wilderness of delights.

MARION HARLAND.

THE GARDENS OF THE PURITAN GRANDMOTHER.

HERE is a great pathos in the fact, that, in so stern and hard a life, there was time or place for any gardens at all. I can picture to myself the little slips and cuttings that had been brought over in the ship, and more carefully guarded than any of the household gods.

I can see the women looking at them tearfully when they came into bloom, because nothing else could be a better reminder of their old home. What fears there must have been lest the first winter's cold might kill them! and with love and care they must have been tended.

. . . Those earliest gardens were very pathetic in the contrast of their extent, and their power of suggestion and association. Every seed that came up was thanked for its kindness, and every flower that bloomed was the child of a beloved ancestry.

SARAH ORNE JEWETT
(From Atlantic Monthly).

CORISANDE'S GARDEN.

"No flowers are admitted that have not perfume," said the duchess to Lothair. "It is very old-fashioned."

 TURN the printed leaves, and fancy brings me,
    Without command,
To where thy garden wondrously enrings me,
    O Corisande!

I tread the turfen terraces, luxurious,
    Its ancient pride,
With golden yew cut into arches, curious,
    Along one side.

And over me and round me float inthralling
    Its perfume sweet,
With sunny sheen and dusky shadow falling
    About my feet.

They call thy garden, Corisande, old-fashioned,
    A garden where
The flowers breathe their lives away, imprisoned,
    To scent the air.

Where woodbines wander, and the wall-flower pushes
    Its way alone,
And where, in wafts of fragrance, sweet-brier bushes
    Make themselves known,

26

With banks of violets for southern breezes
　　To seek and find,
And starred and trellised jessamine, that pleases
　　The summer wind.

And here the flowers' queen, in perfect beauty
　　And calm repose,
Leads a soft life of perfume, with one duty, —
　　To be a rose.

And clove-carnations overgrow the places
　　Where they were set,
And mist-like in the intervening spaces
　　Creep mignonette.

With purple stocks, in sudden breezes swerving,
　　And lilies white,
As if their lifted petals tender curving,
　　Held heaven's light.

And tangled wantonly, together growing,
　　Are frail sweet-peas ;
And all above them, ever coming, going,
　　Communist bees.

O sunlit, soft-hued place for love and lovers !
　　In all thine air
Some reminiscence of lost Eden hovers
　　And makes thee fair.

* * * *

London Society.

HANNAH'S FLOWERS.

ID you ever have an old-fashioned flower-bed in a country garden, — a long, narrow strip of mellow earth, sown crosswise in rows, with various kinds of seeds? You sprinkle these seeds in little furrows a foot apart, pat a thin layer of earth over them, and wait. After a warm shower some late May morning, you find your bed full of ridges, with here and there a crack. In a few hours these cracks have run along the ridges, and from them spring a host of tiny leaves, most of them in pairs. You can almost see them grow."

I do not see such roses now, so full of scent, so deep-dyed, as the double damask and white ones which blossomed in my grandmother's garden. It seems as if they must have gotten their strength from the rugged soil. The damask ones were like peonies for size; and their bushes, thick with full-blown flowers and buds, in every stage of opening, were only surpassed for beauty by those of the creamy-white rose, which were as soft-tinted as the first blush of dawn, and daintily scented as the quickening breath of spring.

Hannah's flowers were all sweet-smelling, gracious, hardy, grateful things. Her pinks were marvels for color and scent. Her bachelor's-buttons, blue and purple and white, perfumed the morning. Her columbines, wild denizens of the garden, kept always a woodland flavor. They got mixed and unsettled as to color, but held fast their untamed nature.

The pride of the garden were the two peony-roots just inside the gate on either side. They were amongst the earliest comers in spring, peeping up out of the brown mould with their great crimson leaf-buds, which speedily thrust up into strong stocks, to be the bearers of as many blossoms. How those peonies grew! New stocks came up every year, and each new stock seemed to bring with it a peony heavier and deeper-dyed than before. Jonathan tied them up every season; but still they waxed bigger and bigger, until a barrel-hoop would not hold them. They were the envy of all the children, and the admiration of farmers' wives.

"E. H. ARR."
(Mrs. Ellen H. Rollins.)

ANIEL WEBSTER always kept his mother's old garden in good condition, ordering his factotum John Taylor to do so, if it required the labor of an extra hand. Till death he loved the flowers that used to bloom there. The common carnation-pink never failed to be acceptable to him on this account, and he always received a bouquet of these flowers with peculiar gratitude. At the time of his great reception in Boston, from the thousands of elegant bouquets showered upon his head as he drove through the streets, a niece of his selected a bunch of carnation-pinks, and presented them to him.

He kissed the hand of the donor, saying, "How fragrant, how delightful, are these little flowers, such as bloomed in my mother's garden!"

Peter Harvey.

A TRIBUTE TO THE SIMPLE NAMES OF OLD-FASHIONED FLOWERS.

URELY there is marked character enough about every plant to give it some simple *English* name, without drawing either upon living characters or dead languages. It is hard work to make · the maurandias and alstræmerias and eschschotzias — the commonest flowers of our modern gardens — look passable even in prose. They are sad dead letters in the glowing description' of a bright scene in June. But what are these to the pollopostemonopetalæ and eleutheromacrostemones of Wachendorf, with such daily additions as the native name of Iztactepoteacuxochitl icohuocy, or the more classical ponderosity of Evisymum Peroffskganum, like the verbum Græcum, Spermagoraiolekitholakanopoledes, — words that should only be said upon holiday, when one has nothing else to do! As to poetry attempting to immortalize a modern bouquet, it is utterly hopeless; and if our cultivators expect to have their new varieties handed down to posterity, they must return to such musical sounds as eglantine and cowslip, cuckoo-pint and primrose, or such as our "plainer sires" gave in larkspur and honeysuckle, ragged-robin and love-lies-bleeding, before bards will adopt their pets into immortal song.

FOUR-O'CLOCKS.

OUR O'CLOCK, the resting-time of the day;
　　Sunlight with shade a fantastic patchwork
　　　weaves,
　　But the shadows lengthen: the wind, while dying
　　　away,
　　Lingers to rustle the quivering aspen-leaves.

I'm under the pear-tree, sitting all alone:
　　My garden is gay with asters, pinks, and phlox,
And many a posy for others' pleasure sown;
　　But here, for myself, I have planted four-o'clocks.

"Old-fashioned," you think, and cannot my choice approve;
　　Rarer blossoms your fancy craves, no doubt;
But, after all, it isn't the flowers we love,
　　But the dear old times that they make us think about.

It's a way they have of making us love them so;
　　We care not long how fragrant and gay they may be;
But deep in our hearts they strike their roots and grow,
　　Tangled and twined with various memory.

H. E. SANFORD.

MISS SEDGWICK'S VISIT TO MISS MITFORD.

HE led us directly through her house into her garden, a perfect bouquet of flowers. "I must show you my geraniums while it is light, for I love them next to my father." The garden is filled, matted, with flowering shrubs and vines. The trees are wreathed with honeysuckles and roses, and the girls have brought away the most splendid specimens of heart's-ease to press in their journals. Oh that I could give my countrywomen a vision of this little paradise of flowers, that they might learn how taste, industry, and an earnest love and study of the art of garden-culture, might triumph over small space and humble means!

AN OLD-FASHIONED GARDEN IN AUTUMN.

HE house stood almost concealed amid a forest of apple-trees, in spring blushing with blossoms, and in autumn golden with fruit.

And near by might be seen the garden, surrounded by a red picket-fence, enclosing all sorts of magnificence.

There in autumn might be seen abundant squash-vines, which seemed puzzled for room where to bestow themselves, and bright golden squashes, and full-orbed yellow pumpkins, looking as satisfied as the evening sun when he has just had his face washed in a shower, and is sinking soberly to bed. There were superannuated seed-cucumbers, enjoying the pleasures of a contemplative old age; and Indian corn nicely done up in green silk, with a specimen tassel hanging at the end of each ear. The beams of the summer sun darted through rows of crimson currants, abounding on bushes by the fence, while a sulky black-currant bush sat scowling in one corner, a sort of garden curiosity.

MRS. H. B. STOWE.

FRANCIS BACON ON GARDENS.

OD ALMIGHTY first planted a garden, and indeed it is the purest of human pleasures. . . . I do hold it, in the royal ordering of gardens, there ought to be gardens for every month in the year, in which, severally, things of beauty may be there in season.

33

I LOVE A GARDEN.

 ND so do I," "and I," "and I," exclaim in chorus all the he and she fellows of the Horticultural Society.

"And I," whispers the philosophical ghost of Lord Bacon.

"And I," sings the poetical spirit of Andrew Marvel.

"*Et moi aussi,*" chimes in the shade of Delille.

"And I," says the spectre of Sir William Temple, echoed by Pope and Darwin, and a host of the English poets, the sonorous voice of Milton resounding above them all.

"And I," murmurs the apparition of Boccaccio.

"And I," "and I," sob two invisibles, remembering Eden.

(What a string I have touched!)

"We all love a garden!" shout millions of human voices, male and female, and juvenile, base, tenor, and treble. From the east, the west, the north, and the south, the universal burden swells on the wind, as if declaring in a roll of thunder that we all love a garden.

THOMAS HOOD.

THE POOR MAN'S GARDEN.

HE rich man in his garden walks,
    And 'neath his garden trees:
Wrapped in a dream of other things,
    He seems to take his ease.

One moment he beholds his flowers,
    The next they are forgot:
He eateth of his rarest fruits
    As though he ate them not.

It is not with the poor man so:
    He knows each inch of ground,
And every single plant and flower
    That grows within its bound.

He knows where grow his wall-flowers,
    And when they will be out,
His moss-rose, and convolvulus
    That twines his pales about.

He knows his red Sweet-Williams,
    And the stocks that cost him dear, —
That well-set row of crimson stocks;
    For he bought the seed last year.

A rich man has his wall-fruit,
    And his delicious vines,
His fruit for every season,
    His melons, and his pines.

The poor man has his gooseberries,
    His currants white and red,
His apple and his damson tree,
    And a little strawberry-bed.

A happy man he thinks himself,
    A man that's passing well,
To have some fruit for the children,
    And some besides to sell.

Around the rich man's trellised bower
    Gay, costly creepers run:
The poor man has his scarlet-beans
    To screen him from the sun.

And there before the little bench,
    O'ershadowed by the bower,
Grow southernwood and lemon-thyme,
    Sweet-pea and gilly-flower,

And pinks and clove-carnations,
    Rich scented, side by side,
And at the end a hollyhock,
    With an edge of London-pride.

And here the old grandmother comes
    When her day's work is done;
And here they bring the sickly babe,
    To cheer it in the sun.

And here, on sabbath mornings,
    The goodman comes to get
His Sunday nosegay, — moss-rose bud,
    White pink, and mignonette.

.   .   .   .

Yes, in the poor man's garden grow
    Far more than herbs and flowers, —
Kind thoughts, contentment, peace of mind,
    And joy for weary hours.

MARY HOWITT.

GRANDMOTHER'S GARDEN.

SUNNY spot of boyhood years
  Was grandma's garden olden:
Its fragrance rare comes floating back
  O'er forty summers golden.

I see the yellow marigold;
  The fringèd "chiny-aster;"
And morning-glories pink and red,
  And white, like alabaster;

The peony, with wealth of bloom;
  The patch of striped grasses;
The four-o'clocks and London-prides;
  And pinks in fragrant masses.

The lilac, standing by the door,
  Was one of that collection,
And always showed a wealth of bloom
  In time of " old election."

The poppy, too, was not forgot,
  Nor crimson prince's-feather:
Oh, what a swamp of beauty rare
  Was growing up together!

And when the early blossoms came
   Our garden-patch adorning,
How joyfully I watched for them
   Each fragrance-laden morning!

All through the long, bright summer days,
   It proved a home of pleasure
For humming-birds and butterflies
   That sought its hidden treasure.

But she who planted them is gone
   Where bright ones greet the comer,
And where the flowers richly bloom
   Through one eternal summer.

CHARLES F. GERRY

Rose Terry Cooke

Lucy Larcom

Edna Dean Proctor

H. H. (Helen Hunt)

Hezekiah Butterworth

Mary D. Brine

Julia C. R. Dorr

Marion Harland.

www.ingramcontent.com/pod-product-compliance
Lightning Source LLC
Chambersburg PA
CBHW030911260626
47169CB00008B/2796